D0058494

While Standing
on One Foot

Nina Jaffe and Steve Zeitlin

While Standing on One Foot

*Puzzle Stories and Wisdom Tales
from the Jewish Tradition*

Pictures by John Segal

Henry Holt and Company • *New York*

We would like to thank City Lore: The New York Center for Urban Folk Culture and Bank Street College of Education for their support throughout this project. David Szonyi reviewed the text for historical accuracy and detail. Peninnah Schram of the Jewish Storytelling Center at the 92nd Street YMHA and Solomon Reuben provided moral sustenance and thoughtful advice. Dov Noy, the renowned Israeli folktale scholar, went out of his way to talk with us and offer suggestions and stories. Our editor, Marc Aronson, nurtured and guided the project wisely at every stage.

For overall inspiration, we owe thanks to our parents and grandparents, aunts and uncles who first handed down this tradition to us. Our children—Ben and Eliza, and Louis—pitted their wits against the sages in the stories and taught us a few things in the process. May the cleverness and ingenuity of these rabbis, the humor of the Chelmites, and the wisdom of these folk stories be with them always.

Henry Holt and Company, Inc., *Publishers since 1866*
115 West 18th Street, New York, New York 10011

Henry Holt is a registered trademark of Henry Holt and Company, Inc.
Text copyright © 1993 by Nina Jaffe and Steve Zeitlin
Illustrations copyright © 1993 by John Segal. All rights reserved.
Published in Canada by Fitzhenry & Whiteside Ltd.,
195 Allstate Parkway, Markham, Ontario L3R 4T8.

Library of Congress Cataloging-in-Publication Data
Jaffe, Nina. While standing on one foot: puzzle stories and wisdom
tales from the Jewish tradition / by Nina Jaffe and Steve Zeitlin.
p.   cm.
Includes bibliographical references.   1. Legends, Jewish.   2. Tales.   3. Literary
recreations.   [1. Folklore, Jewish.   2. Literary recreations.]   I. Zeitlin, Steven J.
II. Title.   BM530.J34   1993   296.1'9—dc20   93-13750

ISBN 0-8050-2594-4 (hardcover)
5   7   9   10   8   6
ISBN 0-8050-5073-6 (paperback)
1   3   5   7   9   10   8   6   4   2

First published in hardcover in 1993 by Henry Holt and Company, Inc.
First paperback edition, 1996

Printed in the United States of America on acid-free paper.∞

For my husband, Bob.

—N. J.

For my wife, Amanda, who in the daily rush of work and children has helped me find the wisdom to appreciate life "while standing on one foot."

—S. Z.

Contents

While Standing on One Foot

Introduction

☞ Have you ever heard the famous story about King Solomon? One day the wise king was approached by two women arguing over a baby. Each claimed the child was hers. Unable to judge, King Solomon thought up a plan—he offered to cut the baby in half, giving half to the one, half to the other. The first woman agreed with Solomon. "Let the baby be neither mine nor hers, but divide it. If I can't have the child," she cried, "she can't have it either." The second woman pleaded with Solomon not to hurt the child. "Give her the baby. I'd rather lose the child than see it slain." Solomon knew immediately that this was the rightful mother. He returned the baby to her.

How many kings, how many princes, how many people could have solved that problem as cleverly as King Solomon? Wisdom stories have been favorites among many cultures throughout the world. In the Jewish tradition, wisdom tales have a special importance. Throughout much of their history, Jews have lived in situations where they were persecuted or were the victims of prejudice and superstition. They have been forced to think fast in many different roles: as prisoners and judges, as husbands and wives, parents and children. In Jewish folktales, time and again, wise people—rabbis and scholars, carpenters and traders, women as well as men—think up ingenious ways of escaping from difficult situations not through violence but through cleverness and cunning.

The stories told in this book come from or are set in many eras in Jewish history. We begin with a chilling tale from medieval times when the Spanish Jews, whose descendants are called Sephardim, were suffering during the Inquisition. "The Grand Inquisitor" is a classic puzzle tale that gives you a chance to match wits with a legendary rabbi from the fifteenth century. Then we take you back to the very early days of Jewish history with a number of stories from the time when many Jews still lived in the area around Israel in the Middle East. Following the route of the Jews when they left the Middle East, we then tell a number of tales about the Ashkenazim, those Jews who lived in Germany and then moved eastward to Poland and Russia in the thirteenth to nineteenth centuries. Many Jews moved to America in the period from the 1880s to the 1920s, and we tell one story from the streets of the Lower East Side, where many of the immigrants settled, and one set in modern-day New York. Many Jews also remained in Europe, and we tell one story set in Hitler's Germany. We end with a classic rabbinic legend, which inspired the title of our book, and finish with a brief epilogue—a story about storytelling. In all of the stories, our heroes and heroines have to draw on their wisdom not only to outwit great villains, but also to solve some of the tough problems of daily life.

In this book, you are invited to match wits with the heroes and heroines in the stories. Read the first part of each story and imagine what you would have done in that dangerous or tricky situation. Then read on to see how the hero or heroine solved the problem or escaped the predicament. (Remember, all of the solutions are peaceful ones, so you can't use violence as a way out.) You may be caught off guard. Like the wise rabbis and clever souls in the stories, you will have to think fast and make quick and wise decisions—"while standing on one foot."

The Grand Inquisitor

✍ For centuries, large numbers of Jewish people lived in the city of Seville in Spain. By 1378, the town had twenty-three beautiful synagogues and had become a center for Jewish learning. But in the fifteenth century, the kings and queens of Spain were trying to unite their land and make it a Catholic country. They forced many Jews to convert to Christianity on pain of death. Some were killed, but others continued to practice their religion in secret. The Spaniards suspected this, and in 1481 they enacted the Spanish Inquisition. The Inquisition gave them the power to investigate these converts, or conversos, as they were called. Any Jews who were still practicing their religion secretly were to be burned at the stake. To put this cruel policy into action, King Ferdinand and Queen Isabella appointed inquisitors all over Spain. More Jews were killed, and in 1492, the year Columbus sailed for America under the Spanish flag, the remaining Jews were expelled from Spain. In 1991 the government of Spain finally apologized to and honored the Sephardic Jews it had expelled five centuries before.

Once, in the city of Seville, a terrible crime was committed and no one knew who did it. Looking around for someone to blame, the Grand Inquisitor decided that the Jews must be at fault. Of all the Jews in Seville, he decided to go after Rabbi Pinkhes, rabbi of the largest congregation in the city. The rabbi was the man the Jews listened to and respected the most. If he was convicted, the Jews would surely suffer. The Grand Inquisitor put the rabbi on trial and tried to convince a jury that he was guilty. The jury told him that there was not a shred of evidence to support his charge. But there was no stopping the Grand Inquisitor. He came up with a new plan to convict the wise man.

"We will put this matter before God," he said. "I have decided that the fairest way to decide this is to draw lots. I will place two rolled-up pieces of paper in a box. One will say 'guilty,' the other 'not guilty.' If the esteemed rabbi picks the piece that reads 'guilty,' it will be a sign that he and all the Jews are guilty as charged. The rabbi will be executed on the spot. If he draws the piece that says 'not guilty,' we will have to let him go."

But the Grand Inquisitor was a wicked man. He wanted to see the rabbi dead, and he was not about to let him go. The rabbi knew this and suspected that the cunning inquisitor would write "guilty" on both pieces of paper.

The Grand Inquisitor laughed wickedly and told the rabbi, "Now, pick one."

If you were standing in the shoes of Rabbi Pinkhes, wise leader of the largest synagogue in Seville five hundred years ago, what would you do? How would you escape from the Grand Inquisitor's wicked trap?

🙰 🙰 🙰

Rabbi Pinkhes knew the Grand Inquisitor well. He understood his devious train of thought. He smiled at the gloating judge. "How kind of you," he said, "to allow me a chance to go free. How fair and just to leave this matter up to God." Then, with a quick motion, he reached his hand into the box, drew a piece of paper, and before anyone could tell what he was doing, swallowed it!

"Why did you do that?" exclaimed the inquisitor.

"Now we will never know which piece of paper you drew. This is sure death for you."

"I was inspired by God to swallow the paper to prove my innocence! If you have any doubt, any doubt whatsoever," said the rabbi, "just look at the piece of paper in the box. If it says 'not guilty,' then the one I swallowed must have said 'guilty.' But if it says 'guilty,' why, that must mean that the one I swallowed said 'not guilty.'"

The Grand Inquisitor gulped. Try as he might, he could not find a reason to disagree. So he reached into the box and read what the piece of paper said. Just as the rabbi suspected, it said "guilty."

"You see?" said the rabbi. "The one I swallowed must have said 'not guilty.'" The Grand Inquisitor's face turned red, but he had to set the rabbi free.

☞ ☞ ☞

Leviathan and the Fox

☙ Leviathan is the Hebrew name for a mythical sea monster who was known by different names throughout the ancient civilizations of the Middle East. It is written in the Torah (the Five Books of Moses) that on the fifth day, God created the fish of the sea, large and small—including Leviathan. There are many rabbinic legends, called Midrash, that have been passed down about this great and powerful creature of the deep. This story tells of one small creature who dared defy Leviathan—the wily fox.

In the beginning of the world, the ancient legends say, it was Leviathan, the great sea monster, who ruled the creatures of the land and sea. He had more than a hundred eyes, and brilliant scales that shone brighter than the sun. One swish of his tail would cause the ocean to boil and churn with towering waves. No weapon on earth could harm him, and even the angels feared him. But there was one creature who was not afraid of Leviathan, and that was the fox. Small though he was, the fox was nimble and quick. Many times he escaped the traps set for him by other animals.

The name of Fox was spread throughout the land until finally it reached the ears of the great and powerful Leviathan.

One day Leviathan called his subjects to appear before him in a great assembly at his undersea palace. He wanted to count all the creatures in his dominion. From mountain and forest, lake and sea, the creatures began to arrive—the sheep, the giraffe, the bald eagle, the flying squirrel, the turtle, and the hare. One by one, they appeared before him. No one dared to refuse. As he counted all who came, he noticed that one creature was missing—Fox.

"Hmm," said Leviathan to himself. "If this animal is so clever, he may be very useful to me indeed. I am strong, it is true, but I wish to have even greater power. Let's say I were to eat the heart of the fox. Then I would be not only the strongest of all living things, but the cleverest as well. I must have him brought to me."

Leviathan sent two of his most trusted servants—

Swordfish and Sea Bass—to find Fox and bring him to the palace. The two fish swam for many miles. Finally they saw a lone figure dancing at the edge of a beach. Since they had never seen a fox before, the two fish approached and asked where they could find him. The dancer told the two fish, "Go to the place where the water meets the land, where you see a fair creature dancing like the wind." They turned to begin the search. But Sea Bass began to think, The place where the land meets the water, a fair creature dancing . . .

"Wait," said Swordfish. "That sounds like . . ."

"You're right," said Fox. "That's me!"

The fish invited Fox down to Leviathan's palace, saying that he would be treated as the king's most honored guest. They cajoled him with sweet words. "Our king has prepared a huge feast for you," they said. "He has heard of your great wisdom and desires to meet you. He respects you so much that he has invited you to remain with him always as his most trusted adviser! Just think—you'll never have to hunt for your next meal again!"

At this thought, the fox was indeed tempted to go with them. "But I cannot swim," he said. "How shall I get there?"

"Oh, that's no problem," Swordfish said, smiling. "Just hold on to my fin and keep one foot on Sea Bass's tail. You'll be safe with us!" Fox was con-

vinced. He jumped on their backs and set off to see Leviathan.

As they swam through the cold waves, with the land receding far behind, he began to feel uneasy about the situation. "Oh, fish," he asked them, "now that you have me on your backs, far from my home, tell me the truth. Why does Leviathan really want to see me?"

The fish had Fox just where they wanted him, and now, with the creature safely on their backs, they had nothing to hide. The fish revealed that their king, Leviathan, wishing to be the cleverest of all creatures as well as the strongest, planned to take out Fox's heart and eat it. "You won't be the guest at the feast," they laughed. "You'll be the first course!" Fox shivered from the tip of his tail to the end of his nose. Is this how my glorious life is to end? he asked himself.

If you were in Fox's place, could you think of a trick to save yourself?

❧ ❧ ❧

Fox thought quickly. Then his eyes lit up. He spoke to the fish very sweetly and said, "My friends, if only I had known what you really wanted, I would have taken my heart with me! As it is, I left it at home."

"What?" cried the fish. "You don't have your heart?"

"Oh, no," replied the fox. "We foxes never travel with our hearts, unless it is for a very important reason. We always leave them at home. I would hate to have you take me all the way down to Leviathan's palace, only for him to find that you did not bring the very thing he asked for! That could make him very angry!" The two fish were terrified. The last thing they wanted was to upset Leviathan. "If you really want to bring Leviathan my heart," continued the fox, "bring me back to shore. I'll be happy to get it for you!"

The fish swam quickly back to shore with their passenger clinging to their fins. As soon as they neared the land, Fox jumped off their backs to safety and began once again to dance on the beach.

"What are you doing?" cried the servants of Leviathan. "This is no time for dancing! Leviathan is waiting! Hurry up and get your heart!"

"Foolish creatures," cried the fox. "How could anybody travel without his heart? How could any animal live one instant without a heart!"

"You've tricked us!" wailed Swordfish and Sea Bass.

"Of course I did," replied the fox. "I've escaped all the traps that have ever been set for me—even by the Angel of Death himself! Did you really think I could be fooled by a couple of silly fish?" And with that, he went dancing off to his secret lair.

The two servants of Leviathan swam back very slowly to tell their master what had happened. He listened to their story, and after scolding them soundly for their failure, he opened his great mouth and swallowed them up.

The Case of the Boiled Egg

🖋 Many Jewish folktales are based upon characters and events described in the Torah and other biblical texts. Characters such as Elijah the prophet, Moses, King David, and King Solomon have been incorporated into Jewish folktales from all over the world. Sometimes when they appear in folktales, these characters bear little resemblance to their biblical counterparts. For example, the biblical Elijah is a strict and forbidding prophet of ancient Israel. However, in Jewish folktales he becomes a beloved figure who appears on earth to help the poor and needy, reward the faithful, and herald the coming of the Messiah. In the Bible, King Solomon, who lived in the tenth century B.C.E., was described as the builder of the Temple of Jerusalem, and was known for his great wealth and many wives. Folktales about

King Solomon, on the other hand, portray him time and again as a wise judge who also possessed many secret powers that enabled him to overcome the forces of evil. The following story is one example of these tales in which, even as a child, Solomon displays his unusual powers of perception and insight.

King David had many attendants and soldiers who served him at his court. One day he sent one of his weavers on a journey to purchase wool for the royal looms. On the way back, the weaver stopped for breakfast at an inn along the roadside. He ordered a boiled egg from a gruff, surly innkeeper. He ate his egg, but when the time came to pay for it, he realized that his pockets were empty—he didn't even have the few coins necessary to pay the innkeeper for the egg.

The innkeeper scolded him for not having the money. The weaver pleaded with the innkeeper and told him that he would pay him back as soon as he could. With the innkeeper still mumbling under his breath, the weaver mounted his mule and returned to the palace. There he was greeted by his friend, Prince Solomon, King David's son, who was just a child at the time.

Since the egg cost only a few coins and the inn was miles from the palace, the weaver didn't return to pay his debt until a year later, when he was on another

journey. This time he brought the young Solomon with
him on his mule. When they walked into the inn, the
weaver observed that the innkeeper was as gruff and
surly as ever.

He approached the unhappy man and said, "I am
here to pay you for the egg that I ate here one year ago."
But when the weaver put the few coins down on the
table, the innkeeper scowled.

"What is this for—a measly two coins!"

"It's for the boiled egg," replied the weaver courte-
ously.

"Is that what you think an egg is worth?" barked the
innkeeper. "If I had not sold you that egg, that egg
would have hatched into a chick. And that chick would
have had a dozen chickens, and each of those chickens
would have had a dozen more. I demand a sum equal to
the worth of all those chickens."

The two argued until it seemed as if they would come
to blows. Finally young Solomon called out, "Let us
take the matter to my father, King David."

When the innkeeper realized that the young boy with
the weaver was King David's son, he quickly quieted
down. They resolved to take the matter to the king.

King David heard both sides of the case and said that
he would render a judgment the next day. But Solomon
and the weaver were worried. King David clearly
thought that the law was on the innkeeper's side.

Solomon snuck back to the weaver's hut behind the

palace to talk with him that night. The weaver was dejected as he sat at his simple wooden table and ate his nightly meal of boiled beans.

"Solomon, what am I to do? I am just a weaver in the king's court. How will I ever get the money to pay the innkeeper for the nearly hundred and fifty chickens that he claims I owe?"

"There must be a way to convince my father that you are right. But what, though?"

Then Solomon had a brilliant idea. "I've got it!" he exclaimed. "The answer is in the beans! The answer is in the boiled beans!"

Can you guess how Solomon persuaded King David that the weaver owed the innkeeper for only a single boiled egg?

🎵 🎵 🎵

Solomon knew that each morning King David came out for a walk in his garden. So the next morning, bright and early, Solomon and the weaver went out with a steaming-hot plate of boiled beans. As the king passed by, they began planting them in the ground one by one. The king stared at them in amazement.

"What do you think you're doing? Whoever heard of planting boiled beans? Nothing can grow from them!"

The weaver replied, "If it's possible to hatch a chicken from a boiled egg, then it's possible to plant crops from boiled beans!"

When he heard this, King David was convinced of the weaver's claim. He ruled that the poor man needed to pay the innkeeper only for the cost of a single boiled egg. The weaver smiled and told King David that the boiled beans had been Solomon's idea. From that day on, King David always asked his son for advice when he had a difficult case to decide, and when he grew older, Solomon's wisdom became known the world over. Perhaps this story also explains the Yiddish proverb *A kindersher saychel iz oychet a saychel.*—"A child's wisdom is also wisdom."

🖌 🖌 🖌

The Court Jester's Last Wish

🙚 Around the year 587 B.C.E., the Babylonians conquered the kingdom of Judah and destroyed the original beautiful temple in Jerusalem built by King Solomon. Many of the Jews were taken to Babylonia as prisoners. Unlike many conquered peoples, the Jews clung to their religion. Inspired by a prophet named Ezekiel, they continued to practice their customs and believe in one God.

Among the many men and women taken prisoner by the Babylonians was a funny young man named Zev Ben Shmuel. Perhaps if this clever soul were alive today, he would have become a stand-up comic. But in those days, he was the court jester for a Babylonian king.

On feast days and holidays, he made the rulers laugh. He told jokes and was merry. Still, Zev Ben Shmuel remained proud of his religion and his heritage. He believed in one God and would not bow before the king's idols or before any man. Once, the king's chief military commander, who hated Jews, insulted him in the hallway of the palace.

"Swine!" the soldier called out.

Without missing a beat, the jester held out his hand. "Pleased to meet you, Mr. Swine. Zev Ben Shmuel, at your service."

This infuriated the commander, who reported the mischief to the king. He demanded the immediate execution of Zev Ben Shmuel. Reluctantly the king agreed.

"But is that fair?" exclaimed Zev Ben Shmuel. "After all those belly laughs I have given you? One bad joke and I'm doomed?"

The king was determined to put through his sentence. "But," he said, "for all the laughter you have brought to me and my court, I shall grant you one favor—I shall let you choose the manner of your death. Hanging, poisoning, being devoured by wild beasts, anything you wish, we shall carry it out."

The jester contemplated his bitter fate. He thought and thought. What manner of death do you think this clever jester chose? What manner of death would you have chosen?

He returned to the king and said very simply, "Old age."

Zev Ben Shmuel, the story goes, lived to a ripe old age, and he never lost his sense of humor. Some say that he was still alive in 538 B.C.E., when King Cyrus of Persia conquered Babylonia and allowed the Jewish exiles to return to Judah, where they built a new temple in Jerusalem.

The Most Precious Thing

🐏 In ancient times, as today, there were many laws
to govern the terms of marriage and divorce. Among
the Jews of first- and second-century Palestine and
elsewhere in the Middle East, a marriage contract was
considered binding. However, if the couple did not
have any children after a certain number of years—
generally ten—the husband could ask for a divorce.
They would still have to go to a rabbi or judge for
permission.

This story has found its way into folktales
throughout the world, but it was included in the
Jewish wisdom literature of the Talmud—the books
of legal discussions and commentary on the laws of
Moses that were written down by rabbinic scholars
many centuries ago.

The city of Sidon, on the coast of Lebanon, was said to be the jewel of the Mediterranean. Sea breezes blew gently through the city's fragrant gardens and cobbled streets. Sidon's ships sailed far and wide, and with their constant trading, the merchants of the city brought spices, cloth, and riches of all kinds back to their home port. The tall cedars of Lebanon gave cool shade to all who traveled there. Fine craftsmen and artisans carved marvelous designs on the doorposts and gateways of its busy streets, which glistened in the light of the radiant sun.

In this fabled city, there once lived a couple who had been happily married for many years. They lived and worked side by side and cared for each other dearly. But as the years went by and no children were born to bless their home, a great sadness fell upon them. By law, they had a right to a divorce. Every year they thought about it. And every year they put off their decision. But finally the husband said to his wife, "We have waited many years, but since fate has not granted us children, I have decided that it is best for us to separate, for I truly want a child. You must go back to your father's house, as the law requires." And the wife, knowing she could not change her husband's mind, agreed to his decision.

The next day, under a cloudy morning sky, they set off to seek the advice of Rabbi Simeon Bar Yochai, who had come to live in Sidon from the holy city of

Jerusalem. Simeon Bar Yochai had traveled to many places, sometimes to study with the great teachers of the region, sometimes to teach at the centers of learning and law. And sometimes he found himself in flight from the Romans, who resented his harsh criticisms of their emperor and imperial governors. In Sidon he enjoyed the warm air and sea breezes, and he was pleased to answer all who came to him for help and advice.

As the couple arrived at his door, Bar Yochai set out two chairs for them in the small inner courtyard of his home, and waited to hear what they had to say.

"Rabbi," began the husband, "my wife and I have been happily married for more than ten years. But we have not been fortunate enough to have children. Now, as the law permits, I have decided that she should return to her father's house. Please grant us a divorce, so that we can separate with honor and dignity."

Rabbi Bar Yochai looked at the couple for a long time. Then he said to them, "My children, I do not like to see you separate, but as the law requires, I give you my permission. I ask only one thing of you both. Before your wife takes her leave of you, have a feast and celebrate together. For just as you rejoiced at your marriage, so should you do the same at the hour of parting." The couple agreed to his terms and set off back to their home sadly, preparing to take their leave of one another.

As they walked through the cobbled streets, the husband turned to his wife and said, "My dear wife, you have been faithful and loyal to me always. Do not go empty-handed to your father's house. When you leave, you must take a gift. Look over all that we own, and choose whatever in your eyes is the most precious thing in our household." With that final word, they opened the door of their house and stepped inside, to do as Rabbi Bar Yochai had bidden them.

The wife knew that she did not want to leave her husband, and that he did not really want to leave her, although fate had not granted their wish to have a child. What could she do to change her husband's mind?

🌿 🌿 🌿

That afternoon the wife went to the marketplace and filled her basket with dates and almonds, pomegranates and spices, and the finest of delicacies. From their wine cellar, she carried out many jugs of their best wine, made from the sweetest grapes in the vineyards of Sidon. As evening fell, she set the table as beautifully as if it were the Sabbath. Her husband ate and drank his fill. Whenever his glass grew empty, she filled it to the brim.

"This is the last meal we shall ever eat together," she

said to him. "Let us enjoy it to the last crumb of bread and the last drop of wine." Her husband continued to eat and drink, but she herself tasted just a little of everything. By the time the sun had set and the moon had begun to rise, her husband, drunk with the wine and sated with the food, fell snoring into a deep sleep.

As soon as she saw this, the wife called one of her servants, who helped put her husband into a wagon. As he lay there on the straw, she rode with him to her father's house, where once again the servant helped her place him on a wooden bed. As dawn broke, the husband woke up from his sleep and looked around him. Nothing looked familiar to him until he saw his wife standing by the bedside.

"Where am I?" he asked. "What am I doing here?"

"Don't you remember your promise to me?" she replied. "You told me before we parted that I could take with me the most precious thing I could find to my father's house. That is where you are now, under his roof. I looked over all that we owned, but I could find nothing as precious as you."

When he heard these words, the husband smiled and said, "You have done wisely, and I have been a fool. Let us return home and continue on as we have always done, happy and content with one another."

And so they did for many years, living and working

together under the sunny skies of Sidon. The Midrash says that when Simeon Bar Yochai heard the news, he went and prayed for them, and some time after, the child they had been hoping for was born. But that is another story.

Benjamin and the Caliph

🍂 In the first century, the Jewish people living in the land of Israel were conquered, and after 135 C.E., were dispersed by the Romans. The communities Jews set up around the world when they left Israel are known as the Diaspora. From that time until very recently, when the modern state of Israel was established, most Jews have lived among other peoples—subject to the rule of governments that often did not appreciate or understand their way of life. In many cases, the Jews were allowed to practice only certain occupations, or were forced to live within restricted areas. The rules under which they lived were unpredictable and constantly changing. In this story, a foolhardy but quick-thinking traveler must adapt quickly to these changing rules—to save his life.

Once, a caliph devised a wicked plan to slay all the Jews in his kingdom and all those who dared to enter its gates. He told his soldiers, "Each time a Jew enters the gates, he must be stopped! Ask him to tell us something about himself. If he lies, take him to the block and behead him. If he tells the truth, take him to the scaffold and hang him! In my kingdom, no Jew will survive!"

At that time in Morocco, there lived a tall, smart, and handsome young merchant named Benjamin, who was determined to explore some business opportunities in the caliph's kingdom. His rabbi and the elders of the community tried to talk him out of it. They knew the wickedness of the caliph. But Benjamin could never be talked out of an adventure. He saddled his mules and set off on the long journey to the caliph's kingdom.

When he arrived at the gate, the soldiers demanded to know his identity. "I am a Jew from Morocco. A traveling merchant," he replied.

"We are under orders from our caliph to ask you a few questions. Tell us something about yourself," they said, laughing. "If it's true, you hang. If it's a lie, we will behead you!"

Benjamin did not have a moment to regret his decision to take this fateful journey. He had to think on his feet. If I tell the truth, he thought, I hang—but if I lie, they'll cut my head off. This could be the end of me. Then he hesitated, smiled to himself, and began to speak.

Can you guess how this clever traveler escaped his fate?

🎐 🎐 🎐

Benjamin the businessman had an inspiration. He shouted out: "Today you will behead me."

When the caliph heard his reply, he laughed aloud. He cried to his men, "Yes! Sharpen the scimitars and sabers! Prepare the block! Today you lose your head!"

"But your honorable caliph," said Benjamin, "if you behead me, that would mean I told the truth."

"Yes, certainly," said the caliph.

"But if I told the truth, that means I should be hanged."

"Precisely," said the caliph. "Soldiers, place your swords back in your scabbards! Hangman, get your noose." Sneering, he thought to himself, Does this man think I really care whether I hang him or behead him? "Over here," he cried. "This is where we hang our prisoners."

Benjamin gazed up at the hangman preparing the

noose on the scaffolding. "But sir," he said, "if you hang me, that would mean I told a lie." Benjamin had found a logical flaw in the caliph's wicked plan.

"Of course," cried the caliph. "Do you think I have no brains?"

"But if I told a lie, I should be beheaded."

"Of course—you told a lie. So, indeed, we'll slice off your head," said the caliph.

"Aha!" cried the Jew. "But now you have a problem. You can't hang me, but you can't behead me either."

The caliph scratched his own head as he thought: This is a difficult matter indeed. This man, this so-called Benjamin, came into my kingdom and said, "Today you will behead me." But if I cut his head off, why, that would mean he told the truth—so I think he should be hanged. But if I hang him, that would mean he told a lie, in which case he should be beheaded—so I cannot hang him, and I certainly can't behead him.

The caliph became hopelessly confused. No matter what he chose, his own soldiers would know he had done the wrong thing. So, he reasoned, I have no choice but to let this clever fool go.

Benjamin the merchant left as fast as his legs could carry him, happy to be alive. He decided this was not the best time to seek his fortune in the caliph's kingdom.

When something is to be decided by flipping a coin,
have you ever thought of saying, "Heads, I win; tails,
you lose"? By playing with logic in this way, you will
always win the toss. The trick Benjamin used to
escape is also similar to an ancient logical puzzle that
goes like this: If a man from Crete says, "All Cretans
are liars," is he lying? . . . Is he?

The Princess in the Mirror

 Like all peoples from India to England, the Jews told and retold fairy tales from generation to generation. They borrowed many plots and characters from the folktales of their neighbors, and yet made the stories their own. The stories were adapted to Jewish settings and to the Jewish calendar, and became a living part of the Jewish oral tradition. This story was originally told to us by the great folktale scholar Dov Noy, Director of the Israel Folktale Archives.

O nce, we are told, in the land of Israel, there lived a beautiful princess with delicate features. She had long, thick, wavy black hair and a wonderful smile. Among the many young men who fell in love with her were three handsome brothers. Often she invited them to visit her in the palace garden, where they regaled her with songs and told her stories of magic and adventure.

When the time came for her to marry, she knew that she would have none other than one of these handsome brothers—but which one? Remembering the fairy tales they had told her, she decided to proclaim a marriage test. Whichever of them brought her the most marvelous gift—an object she would value above all other things—would have her hand in marriage.

The three brothers, who were best friends, talked among themselves. They knew that only one of them would win her hand. They wished one another luck and agreed that before they presented the princess with their gifts, they would meet back at their home to show one another the presents they had found in the far corners of the world.

The brothers parted, and they traveled around the known world. One brother went to Asia. He wandered through many strange and wonderful cities. He searched among the side streets and bazaars, dazzled by the silk and satin cloth and woven tapestries in the markets. But he found nothing that was sure to win the heart of the princess. Then an old man showed him a magic carpet that would transport him any place he wanted to go. Immediately he paid the price and set off for home.

The oldest brother found his way to Egypt, where he met a magician who had once worked for the pharaohs. "There are many wonders in Egypt," said the magician, "but none as great as the one that I can show you." He held up a shiny glass. "This is no ordinary mirror. Think of a place you wish to see, then look." The oldest brother looked in the mirror. Instead of his face, he saw a land he had only dreamed about but never hoped to see. He thought, This will surely please the princess above all other things. At once he bought the magic mirror and set his course for home.

The youngest brother traveled the lands of Arabia, to the beautiful orchards of Babylonia, where the Garden of Eden is said to have been. In that ancient land, magic fruits abounded, fruits that would make you tall or strong or very wealthy. There he met a farmer tilling the land where it was said Adam and Eve had lived. The brother told him about the beautiful princess.

The farmer took him out to a corner of his farm where, from a small and lovely tree, hung a single apple. "This," the farmer told him, "is an apple that once grew in the Garden of Eden. It is forever ripe, and it was not tainted by the serpent, or by Adam and Eve when they bit into the apple of sin. This is an apple that will cure any illness or heal any pain. Be careful when you choose to use it, for its magic will work only a single time." The youngest brother offered the farmer his entire fortune for this fruit. The farmer considered. He thought, The apple can make only one person better, while his fortune would make my whole family rich. When the youngest brother started home, he had the magic apple safely in his traveling bag.

The three brothers met back at their home. They reveled in their prizes and spoke of their adventures. Again they wished one another luck, knowing that only one of them would be chosen by the princess. Then the youngest brother suggested that they try out the magic mirror. "Why—what would we want to see?" asked the oldest.

"Let's look for the princess," said the youngest. When they looked into the magic mirror, they did see the princess, but she was pale and thin and frail. A crowd of family members hovered over her, weeping. Tears sprang to the three brothers' eyes. Their true love was dying.

The second brother thought of his present. Quickly they mounted the magic carpet, and it whisked them across the kingdom to the palace where the princess lay. When they came to her bedside, the youngest brother took the magic apple from his bag. "Here," he said, "this will make you better."

The princess bit into the apple, and magically, as they watched, the color returned to her face, the red to her cheeks. The brothers and her family gave thanks to God. She sat up in her bed and was healed.

The next day, the princess felt so well she came out

into the garden. Each of the brothers told the story of how he had saved her life. The oldest brother told of how he purchased the magic mirror—without it, they would never have known she was dying. The second brother told about buying the magic carpet at a flea market in Asia—without it, he said, they never would have gotten to her bedside. Then the youngest brother told about the farmer he visited near the site of the Garden of Eden. He told her the story of the magic apple and how its powers healed her. Without it, she surely would have died.

Then the oldest brother asked whose hand she would accept in marriage.

If you were that beautiful princess, whom would you choose?

✄ ✄ ✄

The princess returned to the palace bedroom and considered the offer of these three handsome suitors. She loved them all—but she could marry only one. When she returned, she embraced the oldest brother and thanked him for saving her life with the magic mirror. Then she hugged the second brother and thanked him for the magic carpet, which had also saved her life.

Then she looked into the youngest brother's eyes and said, "I have chosen you. For the magic mirror performs its magic as often as you need it—for me or anyone. The carpet will help anyone to fly. But the apple can be used only once. You could have saved it for yourself, for one day you will need it too, but you gave it to me." Then the beautiful princess kissed the youngest brother. Soon they were married, and lived in happiness and contentment, telling each other stories till the end of their days.

What Is Talmud?

🖝 Rabbi Meir of Rothenberg, who lived in the thirteenth century, was one of the most renowned scholars of his time. As a leader of the Jewish community, he was always being called upon to resolve legal questions or defend his fellow Jews. In this story, set in medieval Germany, a seemingly simple question has a not-so-simple answer. See if you can do as well as Rabbi Meir's studious daughter when she asks him, "How do you study the Talmud?"

R abbi Meir of Rothenberg sat at his desk studying the Holy Books. The morning light streamed through the window, casting a golden glow on the high wooden shelves and leather-bound volumes that covered the walls of his room. As he pondered over the meaning of the words that lay before him, he heard a knock on the door.

"Who is there?" he asked, and smiled when he heard the reply. It was his youngest daughter, Rachel, coming to see him for a morning visit.

Rabbi Meir held out his arms as the young girl ran to greet him. Rachel was a curious child. She was bright and quick, and showed wisdom beyond her years. On her own (for it was not usual for girls to study the Torah in those days), she had learned to read in Hebrew and Aramaic. She knew all the prayers for weekdays, Shabbat, and the holidays, and could recite whole passages in the Torah from memory. But Rachel knew, as did all the children in her family, that the most difficult challenges of all were to be found in the study of the Talmud. Most of all, Rachel wanted to join with her father in that study, but girls almost never had that chance.

Standing next to Rabbi Meir's chair, she asked him, "Father, teach me, how do you study the Talmud?"

In the quiet of the study room, he answered, "Talmud is very difficult. It requires that you not only read and memorize, but also that you think."

"Please, Father," Rachel begged, "let me try!"

"Very well, my daughter. I will give you a lesson. Now, listen carefully. Two men working on a rooftop fell down through the chimney. When they landed on

the floor, one had a clean face, and one had a dirty face. Which one went to wash his face?"

The answer to this question may seem obvious, but is it? What do you think?

∽ ∽ ∽

Rachel puzzled for a moment to herself. The dirty one, of course. Everyone washes his face when it's dirty, right?

But then she had a second thought and said eagerly, "I know, Father. The one with the clean face went to wash!"

Rabbi Meir said, "And how do you know that is the answer?"

Confident now, Rachel replied, "Because he looked at the dirty face of his friend and thought that his must be dirty too, whereas the dirty one looked at the face of his friend and thought that his face must be clean!"

Rabbi Meir smiled at his daughter. "That is good thinking, my child," he said, "but to study Talmud you must think a little harder than that."

"Why, Father?"

"Because," said Meir, as he stroked her hair, "if two

men fall down a chimney, how is it possible that only one of them would have a dirty face?" Rachel's face fell when she heard the reply, but her father consoled her: "You did very well. Always look for the question behind the question. That is how we study Talmud."

And with that idea to think about, Rachel returned to her reading for the day, while her father, Rabbi Meir the scholar, went back to the difficult passage of Talmud that lay before him, to study, to question, and to write.

𝕤 𝕤 𝕤

Throughout most of Jewish history, the study of Talmud was reserved for only men and boys. Very few women even learned how to read Hebrew, which was necessary for religious study. But there have been notable exceptions. One of the most famous and well-respected scholars of her time was Beruriah, the wife of another Rabbi Meir, who lived in second-century Palestine. In recent years, many more women are establishing schools and devoting themselves to the study and understanding of the Talmud.

The Shepherd's Disguise

～ This story comes from a very old collection
called *The Ma'aseh Book,* which was published at the
turn of the sixteenth century in Germany. The book is
a compendium of fairy tales, folktales, and rabbinic
legends that were popular in the Jewish community at
the time. The story of a lowly person who disguises
himself to answer a king's questions was widespread,
and countless variations of the tale can be found
throughout the countries of Europe.

There was once a king who had among his court
advisers a counselor named Kunz. In truth, no
one knew how Kunz ever got into the position of royal
adviser to the king, for he was far from wise. All day
long, he would walk around the palace, listening to

gossip or eavesdropping on important meetings. But he was also ambitious. The other counselors would spend hours working on a problem, but it was always Kunz who got to the king first, saying that the answer to the problem was *his* idea. Naturally, he was a great favorite with the king, but his fellow counselors were getting tired of him and the way he always took credit for things he hadn't done.

One day the royal counselors waited for Kunz to take a walk outside the palace. Then they gathered together to talk over what to do about him. They were tired of his pandering to the king while they did all the work.

"Why don't we tell the king the truth?" said one. "We'll tell him that Kunz has never had an idea in his life. All the wise advice he gives, he hears from us and passes it on, like a parrot!"

So the counselors, in agreement, went to tell the king. At first he didn't believe them. "What can you be saying?" he exclaimed. "Why, Kunz is my most honored friend and counselor. He has never failed me once! He always is the first to give me good advice. But just to satisfy you, I'll put him to a test, and I know he'll come up with a solution on his own, as he always does."

The next day the king called Kunz to the throne room and said, "Kunz, my dear friend and counselor, I have three very important questions that require your expert opinion. If you can give me an answer, I will reward you richly. But remember, I put these questions to you in strictest confidence. Keep them a secret. I want no one to know of our discussion."

Kunz was all too happy to have so much attention from the king, and he was looking forward to his reward. Now he could really lord it over his fellow advisers!

"Just fire away, Your Highness. You know it always gives me pleasure to solve your problems."

"Very well," said the king. "Here are my questions. The first thing I'd like you to tell me is what is the difference between a rising sun and a setting sun? I've always wanted to know. The second question I have for you is how far are the heavens from the earth? And the third question, which I'm sure you'll be able to answer easily, is this: what am I thinking?"

Kunz stammered. "Y-your Majesty," he said. "I need time to ponder these very puzzling matters. Give me three days, and I will return with the answers."

The king was pleased. "But remember, Kunz," he said. "I need to have the answers from you only. You are to discuss these matters with no one, or things will not go well for you!"

Kunz stepped outside. He was shaking like a leaf. He knew he could never answer those questions on his own. He had to get help from somewhere!

"I'll go for a walk in the country," he muttered to himself. "Maybe I'll see someone who doesn't know me. I'll ask him the questions, and get his ideas. If I don't come up with the right answers in three days, I'm a cooked goose!"

So Kunz set off into the countryside. He was wearing his royal cloak and garments—his pride and joy—which shimmered in the morning sun. He walked and walked, past fields and forest, but saw no one on his way. As he walked, he asked the king's questions over and over to himself in a muffled voice. "What is the difference between a rising sun and a setting sun? How far are the heavens from the earth? What is the king thinking?"

Suddenly he heard someone whistling. He looked up and saw a shepherd tending his flocks. The shepherd called him over. "I say," said the shepherd. "I heard you muttering to yourself, and I couldn't help wondering if you needed any help?"

"I most certainly do," said Kunz. "I am a royal adviser to the king. I must give him the answers to these questions, or things will not go well for me—and I only have three days to do it."

"Well, now," the shepherd said. "I might be able to help you out. I heard the questions as you walked along. Why don't you just lend me your royal cloak, while you take my jacket and stay here with the sheep? I'll go over to the king and try to give him the right answers. As soon as he's satisfied, I'll come back and we'll switch places again. You'll return to the palace safe and sound!"

Kunz liked this idea. If the shepherd failed, the king's punishment would fall on *his* head. If he succeeded, then Kunz would go back to the palace, and no one would be the wiser.

So Kunz changed places with the shepherd.

As soon as he arrived at the palace, the shepherd, dressed in Kunz's garments, requested an audience with the king. When he appeared before him, he bowed and said, "Your Highness, I have thought long and hard, and I have come up with the answers to your questions."

"Well," said the king, for he was anxious to prove his other counselors wrong, "tell me what you have discovered!"

How did the shepherd answer the king's three questions?

🦢 🦢 🦢

"Your Highness, we'll take this one step at a time. Your first question was what is the difference between a rising sun and a setting sun? The difference between a rising sun and a setting sun is—the whole world."

The king nodded thoughtfully. That seemed reasonable enough—the sun rises on one side and sets on the other, with the world in between. "Go on, Kunz, my wise and faithful counselor," he said.

The shepherd continued. "Your second question was how far are the heavens from the earth? I have pondered this, and here is my answer. The heavens are as far from the earth as the earth is from the heavens." Again the king nodded in agreement.

"As to your last question, that is the easiest one of all. You asked what you, the king, are thinking. And my answer is this. Right now, you are thinking that I am Kunz, your royal counselor. But in fact, I am the shepherd who tends your sheep in the pastures below!"

When the king heard the shepherd's story of how Kunz had agreed to change places with him, he decided to keep the shepherd on as his royal adviser and leave Kunz in the fields with the sheep. The shepherd got along well with the other counselors, who soon learned to respect his opinion on many matters. As for Kunz, he stayed on happily enough with the sheep, to whom he freely gave his advice and borrowed wisdom at every opportunity.

Hershel and the Nobleman

🖝 Hershel of Ostropol was a real person. He was born in Ukraine, in Eastern Europe, in the middle of the eighteenth century. By that time, most European Jews had migrated from Germany and France to escape persecution. They resettled and now lived in cities, towns, and villages across Eastern Europe. Life under the czars of Russia was especially hard, but Hershel somehow found a way to survive and laugh at his troubles, even in the hardest of times. Hershel was so well known among his people during his own lifetime that even after his death, the accounts of his adventures were told and retold. To this day, Hershel of Ostropol appears in new stories, as well as in the folktales and legends that carry his name.

Hershel was worried. Living in Ukraine was always difficult, especially for a poor Jew with a wife and children to keep clothed and fed. But this year, things seemed worse than ever. All his usual friends and acquaintances in Ostropol (even the wealthy ones) had little food or money to spare. At home his children were hungry and his wife was complaining bitterly.

"Hershel," she said, "why don't you go find a job? Do something to help us, or we won't have a roof over our heads for much longer!" Hershel was in despair.

Then one day, by chance, he heard in the marketplace that a nobleman who owned a country estate nearby was looking for a cook. Hershel had never cooked a day in his life, but that didn't stop him. Immediately he paid the nobleman a visit.

When he reached the estate, the nobleman looked him over carefully and decided to hire him. "But remember," he said, "I expect only the utmost honesty from all my servants. Any wrongdoing and it's off to prison for you!"

Hershel agreed and proceeded down to the kitchen. The first meal that the nobleman ordered him to cook was a roast goose. He was having guests that night, and he wanted them to be well served.

A goose, thought Hershel. I can probably cook a goose. I've seen my wife put a scrawny chicken in the oven, when we've been lucky enough to find one. Roasting a goose can't be that different. Hershel plucked the goose, cleaned out the gizzards, and put a little salt and parsley on it before putting it into the oven. As the goose roasted in its baking pan, a delicious smell began to seep out into the kitchen. Soon it filled the entire room. When he pulled the delectable goose from the oven, he was overcome with pangs of hunger.

Hershel tried to control himself, but he hadn't eaten a full meal in weeks! As soon as he put the goose on the table, he carved off one of the drumsticks and ate it, enjoying every morsel.

Later that night when dinner was served, the nobleman noticed that one of the goose legs was missing. He demanded to see his new cook. "What is the meaning of this!" he roared.

Hershel knew that his job and maybe even his freedom were at stake. He explained carefully, "Sire, is it possible, could it be that this goose had only one leg?"

"Ridiculous!" said the nobleman. "There is no such thing as a one-legged bird! I've a mind to send you to prison for lying and stealing!"

"Please, sire," said Hershel. "Give me a chance to prove I'm right. Give me some time to clear my name. If I don't succeed in convincing you, you can punish me as you see fit."

"I'll give you twenty-four hours," said the nobleman. "Now be off with you!"

Hershel knew he could be facing a fine and many days in jail if he couldn't prove his point. He certainly couldn't tell the nobleman the truth about what had really happened to the goose leg, or he would be in even worse trouble. How did Hershel get out of this jam?

🍂 🍂 🍂

Hershel tossed and turned all night, racking his brain for a solution, but no ideas came to him. Finally, just before dawn, he came up with a plan. The next day, Hershel invited the nobleman to go with him on a hunting expedition. As they trotted down the road through the estate, they saw a stork standing on one leg by the riverbed.

"There!" said Hershel, for this was the moment he had been hoping for. "I told you there was such a thing as a bird with one leg!" Immediately the nobleman clapped his hands and shouted, and the stork flew away, with its two legs stretched out behind.

"Hershel, you are wrong. That bird had two legs. I am going to throw you in prison!"

Hershel kept calm and coolly replied, "Aha! If you had clapped your hands and shouted at the roast goose, you would have seen its other leg too!"

At this, the nobleman burst out laughing. He was so pleased with Hershel's answer that instead of sending him to prison, he sent Hershel home with another roast goose for himself and his family. Hershel never did cook another meal for the nobleman, but they remained friends for many years afterwards. They say, the story of Hershel and the goose leg soon became a favorite for all the people of Ostropol.

The Wise Fools of Chelm

All through Jewish history, wise rabbis have
reasoned their way around difficult religious
questions, wise merchants have found ways to survive
even when the laws were turned against them, and
wise women have found ways to raise their families
in hard times. But of all these wise souls, none
thought themselves wiser than the fools of Chelm.
Chelm is a real town in Poland, but it holds a special
place of honor in the world of Jewish folklore and
legend. The Chelmites were famous for their foolish
wisdom, for in Chelm, wisdom was turned on its
head.

For instance, for the Chelmites, nothing
represented wisdom as much as a long beard. Once, a
clean-faced Chelmite went to the wise and bearded
rabbi to ask why he couldn't grow a beard. The rabbi

answered quite simply that it was a matter of heredity. "If your father couldn't grow a beard, you can't grow one either." "But," said the peach-faced Chelmite, "my father did have a beard!" "Aha," said the rabbi, "that means you must take after your mother." The Chelmite walked away, smiling. The rabbi was absolutely right. It was true, his mother didn't have a beard, and he had been granted a measure of Chelm's foolish wisdom.

Once, in Chelm, there was a wise fool named Shmuel, who was a great lover of riddles and stories. One day, while visiting the town of Berditchev, he stopped by the shul (synagogue) to visit the shammes (caretaker), who was always a source of gossip and tales. On this visit, he was not disappointed. The shammes of Berditchev asked him to ponder this riddle: I am my father's son, but I am not my brother. Who am I?

What a wonderful riddle! Shmuel stroked his long, narrow beard and furrowed his brow. He repeated the question aloud again and again, as if to help it make its way through his ears toward the general direction of his brain: "I am my father's son, but I am not my brother. I am my father's son, but I am not my brother. I am my father's son, but I am not my brother."

Can you figure out the answer to this riddle?

🖙 🖙 🖙

"Can't you see?" said the shammes of Berditchev. "It's me! You see, I am my father's son, but I am not my brother."

Even though he hadn't solved the riddle, Shmuel was very impressed. He hurried back to Chelm, barely able to contain his excitement about telling a new riddle to the wise fools of Chelm.

As soon as he was back in town, he hurried to his fellow Chelmites. He asked them: "I am my father's son, but I am not my brother. Who am I?"

A Chelmite answered, "He is his father's son, but he is not his brother." Then a chorus of voices repeated the question to one another and themselves. The synagogue was abuzz with puzzlement. "I am my father's son, but I am not my brother. I am my father's son, but I am not my brother. I am my father's son, but I am not my brother."

And then, almost in chorus, they looked at Shmuel and said, "We give up. Who is it?"

"Why, of course," he cried, "it's the shammes of Berditchev!"

"The shammes of Berditchev?" they cried.

"Why, yes—he told me so himself!" said Shmuel.

* * *

The struggles of Jewish life gave birth to a special brand of humor—the sense of humor that created the imaginary fools of Chelm—some say in partnership with God. For they say that when God created humans (according to another Chelm story), He wanted to distribute the wise and the foolish souls evenly across the planet. Many people complained that Chelm got more than its share of foolish souls. The truth is, there were plenty of foolish souls to scatter almost everywhere else. For, as we know, there is a little foolishness in every wise person and a little wisdom in every fool.

The Clever Coachman

In Russia at the turn of the century, most Jews lived in shtetls (towns) to which they were restricted by an edict of the czar. Many people spent their whole lives in these towns, never leaving from the moment they were born to the day they died. But there were also many itinerant, or traveling, Jews. Among them were the Jewish musicians called klezmers, who traveled to different towns to play for weddings and celebrations. They sometimes traveled with gypsy musicians, and developed a style of music now called klezmer music. And then there was the maggid, the traveling inspirational preacher. He went from town to town delivering sermons and telling religious stories. He often put up a sign on the synagogue door announcing THE GREAT MAGGID WILL COME HERE TO SPEAK. After each of his talks, he would collect money from the listeners. Some of the maggids were terribly dull, and the boys in the synagogue would argue and play until he could hardly hear himself talk. But if he was good, they would speak about his stories for weeks to come.

———————————————————————

The great maggid of Lublin was among the most famous of speakers in all of Russia. He knew almost everything there was to know about the Torah and about all aspects of religious life. He traveled from town to town giving sermons and taking questions from the audience. He was one of the most learned men of his time, and he was admired by everyone, especially by his coachman, who drove him from town to town.

After many years, the coachman, who had learned the rebbe's sermons by heart, said to him, "I have been listening to you for almost twenty years. I think I could recite your sermons in my sleep. Just once, I would like to change places with you. For one day, I'd like to dress in your clothes and play the part of the wise maggid. Tomorrow we are going to a town where we have never been. Why don't we trade places? I'll be the learned maggid. I'll wear your broad hat and your caftan robe, and you can dress as the coachman. Who will ever know?"

"But what if they ask you questions?" said the great maggid of Lublin.

"For twenty years, we have traveled together. I will answer them just as you would."

The maggid had a big heart and a good sense of humor, and so he agreed. They changed clothes, and when they pulled into the town, the coachman delivered a sermon worthy of the great maggid. Outside the small synagogue, the maggid fed the horses and listened to his own sermon being delivered through the open doorway.

Afterwards the congregation began to ask questions. One by one, the coachman answered them with ease. Outside, the maggid in the coachman's clothing heard the answers and smiled to himself. His coachman had learned well. But then a bookish yeshiva student raised his hand and asked a question no one had ever asked before. The driver did not know the answer. There was a moment of silence. Outside, the great maggid chuckled to himself. "My good coachman is in trouble now."

Can you guess what the clever coachman said? How would you have wriggled your way out of that tight spot?

🦋 🦋 🦋

"Aha," cried the coachman dressed as the great maggid. Then in his most imposing voice, he said, "I cannot believe that this young man has chosen to ask me such a simple question. Why, that question is so simple even my driver outside in my coach, a poor, hardworking man who never set foot in a religious school or yeshiva, can answer it. My dear sir," he called to the driver outside. "Come in, come in and answer this simple question!"

And of course the great maggid of Lublin answered it perfectly.

✦ ✦ ✦

Prince Rooster

🐦 "Many people believe," said Rabbi Nachman from the town of Bratslav (then in Russia, now in Ukraine), "that stories are told to put people to sleep; I tell mine to wake them up." Rabbi Nachman, one of the most famous of all the Hasidic rabbis and storytellers, lived two hundred years ago. He was known far and wide for his stories—and his laugh. His wasn't an ordinary laugh, but a wild and crazy howl. He loved to tell stories about people who had gone mad. In one, the food supply of an entire kingdom was contaminated or poisoned, so that anyone who ate from it was sure to go crazy. The king put his arm around his counselor and suggested that a "seal of madness" be affixed to both their foreheads—this way even after they went mad, they would know they were mad! In a variation of this story, the king tells his best friend and closest adviser that he—the king's trusted counselor—should be the only one not to eat the contaminated food. That way he could travel through the countryside as the one sane and normal person left, crying, "Don't forget, you were not always crazy!"

Rabbi Nachman's most famous story is about a prince who thought he was a rooster.

Once, in an ancient kingdom, there lived a fine and handsome and intelligent prince. But one day he got it into his head that he was a rooster. At first the king believed this was simply a passing thought, a phase his son was going through. But when the prince took off all his clothes and began flapping his arms and crowing like a rooster, the king knew he had a real problem. The prince took up residence under the dining-room table and would eat only kernels of corn dropped onto the royal carpet.

The king was sad to see his son in such a state. He called in his best doctors, his miracle workers, his magicians. One by one they talked to the prince, tried medicine and magic. But he remained convinced that he was a rooster. One by one they filed out. Each time, the rooster crowed.

The king fell into a deep depression, convinced that no one could cure his son of his strange malady. He told his servants to allow no more medicine men or fortune seekers into the palace. He had had enough.

One day an unknown sage approached the palace and loudly knocked upon the palace gate. The king's chief servant cracked open the wooden door and saw an old man with piercing eyes staring at him. "I understand the king's son believes he is a rooster. Well, I am here to convince him otherwise."

The servant slammed the large wooden door. "So many have tried and failed. Go away, old man!"

The next day, the servant heard once again a loud knock upon the gate. Again he cracked open the door. "I have a message for the king," said the unknown sage.

"What is it?" said the servant. "Give it and be gone."

"Tell the king these words exactly: 'To pull a man out of the mud, sometimes a friend must set foot into that mud.'"

The servant had no idea what it meant, but he left the sage waiting outside the gate and took the message to the king. Slumped on his throne, the king listened to the cryptic message. "To pull a man out of the mud, a friend must set foot into that mud." Hmm, what did he mean by that? But as he thought about it, the words began to make sense. He sat straight up and said, "Yes, bring him in. I will give him a chance!"

What was the meaning of the sage's message? How do you think the wise sage cured Prince Rooster?

To everyone's amazement, the wise man began by taking off all his clothes. The king shook his head. Now there were two naked men under the dining-room table, crowing like roosters.

Soon the prince said to the wise man, "Who are you, and what are you doing here?"

"Can't you see?" said the sage. "I'm a rooster, just like you."

The prince was happy to have found a friend, and the palace resounded with flapping and crowing. But the next day, the wise man got out from under the table, straightened his back, and stretched.

"What? What are you doing?" asked the prince.

"Not to worry," said the sage. "Just because you are a rooster doesn't mean you have to live under a table." The prince admired his friend, so he tried it. It was true. A rooster can stand and stretch, and still be a rooster.

The next day, the sage actually put on a shirt and a pair of pants.

"Have you lost your mind?" asked the prince.

"I was a little chilly," said the sage. "Besides, just because you are a rooster doesn't mean that you can't put on a man's clothing. You still remain a rooster."

Puzzled, the prince reluctantly tried on some clothes. The sage then asked for a meal to be served on the golden platters of the king. He sat down with the prince, and without realizing it, the prince began to eat. The sage engaged him in a lively conversation about the affairs of the kingdom. Suddenly the prince jumped up from the table and cried, "Don't you realize that we are roosters? How can we be sitting at this table eating and talking as if we were men?"

"Aha!" cried the sage. "I will now tell you a great secret. You can dress like a man, eat like a man, and talk like a man, but still remain a rooster."

"Hmm," said the prince. And from that day forward, he behaved just like a man. In a few years, he assumed the throne. He led his kingdom to great glory. But every once in a while, the thought occurred to him that he was, in fact, still a rooster—and when he was all alone he would crow a little bit, just to make sure.

🐓 🐓 🐓

On the Streets of the Lower East Side

🐟 In the late nineteenth and early twentieth centuries, waves of Jewish immigrants poured through Ellis Island into America. Like many other immigrant groups, they made the long and dangerous voyage to escape poverty and persecution in their homelands. On the Lower East Side, where many immigrant families started their new life, the Jews were very poor. The writer Harry Golden remembers that his mother would walk from her house on Eldridge and Rivington streets to the market under the Williamsburg Bridge, over a mile each way, just because butter was one penny less there—just one penny less.

In the hubbub of the pushcarts and store owners, there were always disputes to be settled. Many Jews turned to the local rabbis rather than the courts to resolve them. This family story is told by Jack Margolin, a retired lawyer living on Long Island, New York.

My father," said Mr. Margolin, "was one of three rabbis who sat as judges on the court, or beth din, as it was called. Their judgments were final, and there was no appeal. So the responsibility for being fair and correct weighed heavily upon them. This is a story my father told me about one of their most difficult cases."

Once a poor woman came running into the rabbis' courtroom, complaining bitterly that she had been shortchanged. She had bought some old clothes from a pushcart for three dollars. She claimed she gave the merchant all her money, a twenty-dollar bill. How much change did she expect? Seventeen dollars. How much did she get? Seven. The rabbis summoned the pushcart owner. He told a different story. He claimed she had given him only a ten-dollar bill. So he gave her seven dollars change. "Was that right?" he asked. Then he answered his own question. "Of course that's right."

The three rabbis met with the merchant and the customer. Both seemed to be fine citizens and good Orthodox Jews. They followed all the practices of Jewish religious life. But the rabbis had to decide

who was telling the truth. It came down to the merchant's word against the customer's. Whose should
they take?

In this day and age, you might resolve the question
by sending them both to court. The customer and the
pushcart owner would each get a lawyer, and there
would be a trial. Each would come up to the witness
stand and swear to tell the truth, the whole truth, and
nothing but the truth.

But this was a panel of rabbis, not an American
court of law. Jack Margolin's father had an idea. It was
an unusual plan, but the rabbis agreed it was worth a
try. He removed a Torah from the ark in the synagogue and placed it on a table in the small, barely lit
Bet Midrash, or study room, adjoining the synagogue.
Then he took a handful of ashes and sprinkled them
on the cover of the Torah. He lit a candle and placed it
in a far corner, so the room was darkened and the
ashes on the Torah could not be seen. With the scene
set, he told the merchant and the customer that they
should go separately into the study room and swear on
the Torah that they were telling the truth. To seal their
oath, each one was to kiss the Torah, as was the
tradition.

*Who was telling the truth? How did the Torah help to
solve the case?*

❧ ❧ ❧

The merchant went in first. After a few minutes, he came out. The woman then went into the room and reappeared in a few minutes. Rabbi Margolin asked both of them if they had kissed the Torah and were prepared to tell the truth. Both said they had. But the woman's face was stained with ashes, while the pushcart owner's face was clean. The truth revealed itself upon their faces. The verdict was announced. The merchant had to return the ten dollars he had shortchanged the poor woman. Without a word, the storekeeper paid.

❧ ❧ ❧

Deciding who is telling the truth is a theme in many of the world's folktales, including Jewish stories. In Russia men often wore large, round, furry hats. Trying to catch a thief, a rabbi went up to a group of men and declared, "I know which one of you did it." "How do you know?" the men asked. "Because the one who did it—his hat is on fire!" One man's face grew redder and redder. Suddenly he reached up and grabbed the hat off his head. "You're guilty!" cried the rabbi.

Jacob's Sukkah

~ Rooftops are magical places. Up on the roof you can look out over the streets, breathe the air, plant a garden, or even raise a flock of pigeons! You can bask in the sun (it's even called "tar beach" in New York), and it's where you can see the moon and the stars in the evenings.

This story takes place during the Jewish harvest festival of Sukkot. The most important custom of this holiday is to build a small hut or booth called a sukkah to commemorate the temporary structures that Jews built in the desert after escaping from slavery in Egypt. In ancient times, when Jews lived as farmers, this wasn't so hard to do—farmers could build the sukkah from the branches and leaves they found in their fields. But for modern Jews living in big cities, keeping the age-old traditions alive poses a special set of problems. In this story, our city-dwelling hero has to find a way to honor the biblical commandment of building a sukkah. And in a crowded city, what better place to find open sky than on the roof?

Once there was a man named Jacob Leibman, who lived in a small apartment on the top floor of a six-story house in New York City. Jacob lived alone, but he had many friends. Neighbors were always stopping by to see him, and children loved to find him at a free moment when he would sit on the stoop and tell them stories about "the old days." "You children don't know," he would say. "In the old days, a hot dog cost twenty-five cents, and you could ride the bus for a nickel!"

Jacob would tell them about playing stickball in the streets. "When a car interrupted our game, someone would yell, 'Hindu, do it again!' Then we'd repeat the play after the car passed by. In those days," he would say, "there were no refrigerators. If you wanted to keep your food cold, you would put it in a big wooden box, an icebox, and get big blocks of ice from the iceman to put inside, so your meat wouldn't spoil. In summer, if you wanted to keep cool, you could sleep on the roof all night long."

Jacob liked to share his holiday traditions with his neighbors and their children too. On Hanukkah, he always passed out dreidels and chocolate gelt. On Passover, out would come the matzah and gefilte fish. He would even invite his friends in for a Seder, and let the children look for the afikoman—the last piece of matzah, which they always found hidden behind the curtains or under the couch in his small living room.

In the whole neighborhood, there was only one person who didn't get along with Jacob. Of course, he didn't get along with anyone else either. That person was the new owner of the building, Mr. Thomas R. Block. If there was ever a leak in the pipes or a hole in the walls to report, Mr. Block was nowhere to be found. But if he saw children sitting on the steps or caught a tenant putting a holiday decoration in his doorway, he was sure to raise a fuss.

One year, as autumn leaves began to tumble from the trees onto the city sidewalks, Jacob began to prepare for Sukkot. He gathered pieces of wood for the sukkah walls. He collected autumn fruits for decorations, and pine branches to cover the top. He brought a table and chairs for the guests he planned to invite, and carried all these things up to the roof of his house. Now, it happened that on the day before the holiday, Mr. Block was paying an unusual visit to the building. As soon as he saw Jacob carrying his leaves and stacks of wood up to the roof, he began to shout.

"Mr. Leibman! I order you to take that garbage off the roof by sundown, or I'll have you evicted! This

kind of thing is illegal—it's completely against building regulations!" And with that, he stomped off.

But Jacob had decided that enough was enough. He was tired of putting up with Mr. Block and his harassment. Besides, Sukkot was an important holiday. Jacob decided, Mr. Block or no Mr. Block, the sukkah must stay up.

The very next day, Jacob found himself in front of a judge, with Mr. Block waving a citation at him.

"Your honor!" he cried. "This tenant is breaking the building code against my specific orders! I can have him evicted!"

The judge looked down at the defendant from her high bench.

"Well, Mr. Leibman, what do you have to say for yourself?"

Jacob had never been in court before, but he spoke up clearly. He told the judge about the sukkah and that it had to be built under an open sky with a covering of pine branches.

"In this city, where else do you have an open sky, except on the roof?" He explained that the sukkah had to stay up for seven days and seven nights.

"Your honor," Jacob continued, "this is the holiday when my people remember how our ancestors wandered in the desert without a real home. It's a biblical commandment to build a sukkah, and I have always kept it. Sukkot starts tonight, right after sundown tonight! Sitting in the sukkah has never caused any problems before—I hope you will decide in my favor." And with that, he sat down.

The judge listened carefully. She knew that the sukkah would do no damage to the building, and that the tenant should be able to observe his holiday in peace. Yet she also knew that the landlord had the city law on his side. She thought for a while, then spoke.

Jacob walked away smiling, and Mr. Block knew there was nothing else he could do—the law had been upheld. What was the judge's decision?

🌿 🌿 🌿

The judge spoke sternly to Jacob and said, "It is true that building a sukkah on your roof is against our city ordinances. You must take it down, or the full force of the law will be brought against you." Mr. Block smirked to himself. Then the judge smiled and looked kindly at Jacob. "Yes, the sukkah must come down. I will give you exactly eight days to comply, and not a minute more!"

🌿 🌿 🌿

A Bird in the Hand

🐦 Walking through the streets of Bremen in the
1930s, it was easy to see signs of the rising tide of
hatred that was sweeping Germany. Everywhere
there were soldiers in brown uniforms, members of
the new National Socialist (Nazi) Party, led by
Adolf Hitler. Swastikas were painted on walls, and
soldiers wore them on their sleeves. Mischievous
children painted them on German synagogues.
Teenagers in the much-hated Hitler Youth brigades
passed by marching in the famous goosestep, kicking
their legs up stiffly as they walked. Until then, many
Jews had done well in Germany and even thought
of themselves as more German than Jewish. But all
that was soon to change.

One gray afternoon, a rabbi walked sadly through the city, where everything was rapidly changing for the worse. He was filled with sorrow at what he thought might lie ahead. He hoped that the young generation would turn away from this Nazi movement that was taking over the country. In an open field, he saw two young men dressed in the dreaded brown uniforms. The rabbi could see the cruel mischief in their eyes as they approached. One of them had his hands cupped, as if he were holding a precious thing that was twitching and turning, struggling to escape. "What do you think I have in my hands?" snapped the young man.

The rabbi glanced at the Hitler Youth's trembling hands. He saw a feather drift gently from between his nervous fingers. "It's not hard to see," the rabbi said, "that you have a tiny bird cupped in your palms."

"Yes," said the young German, his lip quivering with anger and contempt. "But is the bird alive or dead? Tell us the right answer and nothing bad will happen to you or to your synagogue."

The wise rabbi realized that if he said the bird was dead, they would release the bird. But if he said the bird was alive, they would certainly kill it. In either case, wrongdoing was certain to befall both him and his congregation—and they would be the very ones responsible! The rabbi saw the history of Jewish people pass before his eyes. How many times throughout history had they been put in a no-win situation? Forced to choose between two dead ends. Like the Jewish men and women who had faced the Grand Inquisitor or the caliph's soldiers, the rabbi seemed to have no way out.

How would you have answered the young tormentor's cruel question?

✺ ✺ ✺

When the Hitler Youth asked whether the bird was alive or dead, you might have answered, "The bird is dead." At least that way you might have saved the life of the bird, even if it only encouraged the young men in their mischief.

But the wise rabbi looked straight into the young man's eyes. "You ask whether the bird is alive or dead," he said. "The answer is in your hands. The answer is in your hands."

✺ ✺ ✺

The answer was in their hands. In the years ahead, many young Germans joined Hitler's armies. Some even participated in the Holocaust that followed— two thirds of all the Jews in Europe were killed. But some Germans sheltered Jews heroically in the years ahead. The answer was in each person's hands. And it is in our hands to treat human beings—and all living things—with kindness.

Hillel the Wise

☛ Rabbi Hillel lived in the first century and was a leader of an important group of scholars and teachers in ancient Palestine known as the Pharisees. The Pharisees believed that the words of the Torah needed to be studied and interpreted in every generation. In this way, the many laws and commandments would have meaning for the Jewish people in their everyday lives. Of all the great rabbis of that time, Hillel was the most beloved by scholars and common people alike. In the many stories and legends about the rabbinic sages that have been passed down, he is the one most remembered as a wise counselor and a patient teacher.

There was once a young courtier in King Herod's palace who made a wager with his friends that he could make Rabbi Hillel angry. He had heard of Hillel and decided that he wanted to see if he was really as wise and patient as everyone said. On the following day, he went to the study house where Hillel was teaching a portion of the Torah.

"Rabbi, Rabbi!" he cried, interrupting the lesson. "Why do the Babylonians have round heads?"

Hillel turned to him and said, "That is because their midwives are not properly trained," and the young man left. But the next day, he came back again and cried out in the middle of a discussion of law, "Rabbi, Rabbi, why do the Egyptians have flat feet?"

And Hillel responded, "That is because they walk for miles along the marshlands of the Nile." Then quietly he returned to his students.

"Wait, Rabbi, I have another question for you!" the young man called out.

Hillel spoke softly. "Ask it, my friend, and I shall try to answer."

"Why do the Numidians have such weak eyes?"

Hillel said, "I'm sure that is because of the harsh wind that blows throughout their land, and the sand that is always blowing into their eyes." And with that, he returned peacefully to the discussion at hand.

But Herod's courtier hadn't given up yet. He had wagered four hundred zuzim with his friends that he could make Hillel angry, and he didn't want to lose his bet. All night he stayed up, until he hit upon a plan.

The next day, he burst through the door of the study house, stood in front of Hillel, and started hopping up and down, saying, "Rabbi, Rabbi, can you teach me the whole of Torah while I stand on one foot?" All of Hillel's students looked up from the text they were reading and stared at the young man. Hopping up and down and repeating the question over and over, he looked like a stork flapping his wings and squawking. They whispered to one another, "We study the teachings of the Torah day in and day out! How can Hillel give him an answer in just a few words?"

If you were Rabbi Hillel, what would you have said?

⋆ ⋆ ⋆

Rabbi Hillel remained unperturbed. He looked straight into the young man's eyes and said, "That which is hateful unto yourself, do it not unto your neighbor. That is the whole of Torah. The rest is commentary. Now go and learn."

The young courtier stood perfectly still. Then he said to Hillel, "I hope there are no more in the land of Israel like you!"

Hillel asked him, "Why is that?"

And the courtier replied in a huff, "Because of you, I have lost a wager of four hundred zuzim!"

Hillel smiled into his beard and said, "My friend, it is better that you should lose a wager than I should lose my temper."

The young man returned to Herod's court, and what happened to him after that is hard to say. But the words of Hillel, the wise and patient teacher, are remembered to this very day.

Many religious traditions have a "golden rule" such as Rabbi Hillel's. The Christian tradition has the teaching "Do unto others as you would have them do unto you," and in the Koran it says: "Repel the evil with what is better, and you will see that the worst of enemies can become the best of friends."

The phrase "while standing on one foot" is still a saying in Yiddish (*af eyn fus*) and in Hebrew (*al regel achat*). Like this story, it means to do something quickly or to do a long and complicated thing in a short amount of time.

Epilogue

    The Baal Shem Tov—the Master of the Good Name—was the founder and spiritual leader of the Hasidim of Eastern Europe. It is said that when he had a problem that he couldn't solve, he would go to a certain place in the forest. There he would light a fire and say a special prayer, and he would find the wisdom he needed.

In the next generation, one of his disciples faced another difficult problem. He traveled to that same place in the forest and lit the fire, but he could not remember the prayer. Yet the fire was enough. He found the wisdom he sought.

A generation later, his son, like those before him, had a troubling issue to face. He also went to the forest, but he could not remember how to light the fire. "Lord of the universe," he said, "I cannot recall the prayer, and I

cannot light the fire. I only know the place in the forest, and that will have to be enough." And so it was.

Many generations later, Rabbi Ben Levi sat in his study with his head in his hand. "Lord of the universe," he prayed, "look at us now. We have forgotten the words to the prayer. We do not know how to light the fire. We cannot return to the place in the forest. We can only tell the story of how it was done." Yet, telling the story gave him all the wisdom he needed.

In these stories, we have shared with you some of the wisdom that has been passed down in the Jewish tradition. It is our way of remembering the fire, the prayer, and the place in the woods. We also left room in them for you to re-create and retell in your own way (just as we have done), for stories change every time they are told by a different storyteller to different listeners. It is our stories that bind us from one generation to the next. It is in story that we can touch and imagine all the other worlds of creation, and it is in story that the wisdom of all traditions can be shared, remembered, and retold.

Glossary

Afikoman—Piece of matzah (unleavened bread) used as the ritual dessert for the Seder meal.

Aramaic—The language spoken by many peoples in Palestine and Babylonia in the first century C.E. Many rabbinic scholars wrote and spoke Aramaic as well as Hebrew.

Ashkenazim—Historically, Jews from North, Central, and Eastern Europe, many of whom spoke Yiddish. Many American Jews are descendants of Ashkenazic Jewish immigrants.

Dreidel—It is a tradition to play a game of chance with this spinning top during the holiday of Hanukkah.

Gefilte fish—Fish delicacy from Eastern European Jewish cuisine often served at Passover meals.

Gelt—Yiddish for "coins" or "money." During Hanukkah, small coins, or "gelt," are given as gifts to children.

Hanukkah—The eight-day Festival of Lights celebrated in early winter to commemorate the Jewish victory over a Syrian-Greek invading army and the rededication of the Holy Temple in Jerusalem that took place in the third century B.C.E.

Hasidism—A spiritual movement of Eastern European Jews that was founded in the eighteenth century by Rabbi Israel Ben Eliezer (1700–1760, approximately), who later became known as the Baal Shem Tov—the Master of the Good Name. Followers of Hasidism continue to practice their way of life today.

Matzah—Flat, crisp unleavened bread, one of the symbolic foods served at the Passover Seder.

Midrash—This term comes from the Hebrew word that means "to explain, to draw out." A midrash is a rabbinic tale or legend used to explain or embellish verses of the Torah.

Numidia—An ancient country on the coast of North Africa that was occupied by the Roman Empire. It is the site of present-day Algeria.

Passover—A spring holiday, also known as the Festival of Freedom, during which the biblical story in the Book of Exodus (the deliverance of the ancient Israelites from slavery in Egypt) is retold and celebrated.

Rebbe—Specially honored spiritual leader or religious teacher.

Seder—The traditional festive meal of Passover, which usually takes place at home with friends and family members. Songs, prayers, and the retelling of the Exodus story are featured in this centuries-old celebration.

Shabbat—In Jewish tradition, the twenty-five-hour period from shortly after sundown Friday to about an hour after sundown Saturday, which is a holy day. It is celebrated with the lighting of candles on Friday night, followed the next day by prayer, study, and rest.

Sephardim—This refers to the descendants of Jews who were expelled from Spain in 1492. Sephardic

Jews continued to honor their unique traditions in the different countries they lived in after the Expulsion, and many continue to speak a language called Ladino.

Talmud—From the Hebrew word that means "to study, to learn," it is the name for the many volumes of laws, commentary on the Torah, as well as dissenting opinions and stories. Originally passed on by word of mouth, these complex laws and legends, which have governed Jewish life for centuries, were written down by rabbinic scholars over a long period of time, starting in the third century C.E.

Torah—The Hebrew name for the first five books of the Bible, also known as the Pentateuch, or the Five Books of Moses. Torah is also used to refer to the other books of the Bible included in the Old Testament, and in some cases, to all of religious Jewish learning and knowledge.

Yeshiva—A school for Jewish learning. In Eastern Europe, families would scrimp and save to enable their sons to enter a yeshiva. Scholarship and education has always been highly valued in Jewish cultures throughout the world.

Zuzim—(plural of "zuz") An Aramaic word for an ancient silver coin. This word can still be heard in the first verse of the traditional Passover song "Chad Gadya": "My father bought an only kid [goat] for two zuzim." This song usually comes at the end of the Seder.

About the Stories

The Grand Inquisitor—This story is included in Nathan Ausubel's classic collection *A Treasury of Jewish Folklore* (p. 36), and it is the story that inspired our book. It seems to embody the wisdom of many Jewish stories in a simple narrative that works as a kind of puzzle the wise rabbi must solve. During the Spanish Inquisition, Jews were often accused or suspected of crimes of which they were innocent. These and other periods of persecution gave rise to many stories in which everyday Jews as well as illustrious rabbis were called upon to defend their community or their faith to figures in power. Another famous story of this type, "A Dispute in Sign Language," can be found in *Folktales of Israel* by Dov Noy (pp. 94–97).

Leviathan and the Fox—The character of the clever fox was a favorite in many rabbinic legends and fables. This

Midrash dates back to at least the first century, when the tiny kingdom of Judea was being overrun by the Roman Empire. Similar versions of the story, also dating back to ancient times, were known in India, China, Korea, and other parts of Asia. It is included in Volume I of *Legends of the Jews* (pp. 41–42) by the great scholar of Midrash and Jewish folklore, Louis Ginzberg.

The Case of the Boiled Egg—This legend can be found in *A Portion in Paradise and Other Jewish Folktales* by H. M. Nahmad (p. 44). Storyteller Peninnah Schram has a version, set in Eastern Europe, in her collection *Jewish Stories: One Generation Tells Another* (pp. 66–72). The clever device attributed to Solomon in this story can also be found in many other riddle tales in oral traditions throughout the Middle East and Europe.

The Court Jester's Last Wish—The story that our version is based on is still told as a humorous anecdote in various traditions. Sometimes it is told about an explorer being put to death by cannibals who ask him how he wants to die. A version set in Baghdad is in Ausubel's *A Treasury of Jewish Folklore* (p. 288). The "swine" jest is one of the most commonly told jokes about a retort to an anti-Semitic remark. It appears in *The Big Book of Jewish Humor* (p. 82) by William Novak and Moshe Waldoks. For this book, we combined and adapted the two anecdotes to the era of the Babylonian exile.

The Most Precious Thing—This story, which dates back to the second century, was first written down in the volume on the *Song of Songs* in the collection of rabbinic legends and sayings called *Midrash Rabbah* (pp. 48–49). It is known that Rabbi Simeon Bar Yochai, who appears in the tale, did actually live for a number of years in the city of Sidon when Jerusalem was under Roman occupation. Perhaps this Talmudic story is based on a true incident in his career.

Benjamin and the Caliph—We adapted this story from a version in Ausubel's *A Treasury of Jewish Folkore* (p. 299), which appears under the title "The Jew and the Caliph."

The Princess in the Mirror—In a corner of the library at the YIVO Institute for Jewish Research in New York City, we were told this wonderful story by the renowned folktale scholar Dov Noy, Director of the Israel Folktale Archives. It is a tale told in many parts of the world with popular motifs such as the search for three magical objects. In his book *Folktales of Israel,* Professor Noy mentions variants of the story ("Who Cured the Princess," pp. 139–42) that were recorded in Turkey, Kurdistan, and Uzbekistan, as well as an

African-American version from the Sea Islands of South Carolina.

What Is Talmud?—Marc Gelb, a folklorist, told Nina his version of this story, which he heard from a family friend in New York City in 1991. Another version has also been published in Ausubel's *A Treasury of Jewish Folklore* (p. 3). It is known that Rabbi Meir of Rothenberg, the thirteenth-century scholar, had among his children several daughters. Otherwise, all aspects of this adaptation are purely of the authors' invention.

The Shepherd's Disguise—An Ashkenazic variant of this story, "The Bishop and Moshke," can be found in *Yiddish Folktales* (pp. 214–15), edited by Beatrice Weinreich of the YIVO Institute for Jewish Research in New York City. The original story, "Kunz and the Shepherd," is in Volume II of *The Ma'aseh Book* (pp. 571–75), translated and edited by Moses Gaster in 1934.

Hershel and the Nobleman—This story is based on a popular folk narrative that can be found in different cultures. An Italian version is included in a famous collection of early Renaissance tales called *The Decameron,* by the Italian writer Giovanni Boccaccio. An

Ashkenazic Jewish version, "Reb Hershele and the Goose Leg," can be found in the collection *Yiddish Folktales* by Beatrice Weinreich (p. 221).

The Wise Fools of Chelm—The Chelm stories are classics of Jewish folklore and have appeared in many collections and retellings. A version of this story appears in *The Feather Merchants and Other Tales of the Fools of Chelm* by Steve Sanfield (pp. 41–43). In his version, Steve Zeitlin was inspired by the way the Chelmites repeat the question to themselves over and over as they try to ponder the answer.

The Clever Coachman—This Hasidic story is most often associated with the maggid of Dubno. Versions of it appear in Ausubel's *A Treasury of Jewish Folklore* (pp. 21–22), and Jack Kugelmass writes about the story in *Miracle on Intervale Avenue* (p. 203). He heard the tale from Moishe Sacks, the unofficial rabbi at one of the last Jewish congregations in the South Bronx.

Prince Rooster—Rabbi Nachman was a Hasidic rabbi and a Jewish mystic who asked that none of his stories be written down during his lifetime (1772–1810). But his true friend and apostle, Reb Nathan of Nemirov, wrote down the stories from memory. They were first published in 1815. The story has been retold by Elie Wiesel in his book *Souls on Fire: Portraits and Legends of Hasidic Masters* (pp. 170–71). A version is also included in Peninnah Schram's *Jewish Stories: One Generation Tells Another* (pp. 291–96).

On the Streets of the Lower East Side—We are pleased to be able to include in this collection of traditional folktales an example of a family story that has also been told across a generation. This family tale was sent in by Jack Margolin to the Legacies Project, which gave us permission to develop the tale for this book. Legacies was a nationwide contest that invited Americans over the age of sixty to write about an event that changed their lives. The contest, founded by the late philanthropist Maury Leibowitz and sponsored by JASA (Jewish Association for the Aged), received more than six thousand entries from across the country.

Jacob's Sukkah—This story of a fair judgment was told among the Jewish communities of the Middle East and has traveled all over the world. It was collected by Dov Noy from S. Hilles of Tunisia, and included in his book on Jewish folktales from Tunisia. A retelling of this version can be found in *Seventy and One Folktales for the Jewish Holidays and Festivals* by Barbara Rush and Dr. Eliezer Marcus (pp. 77–78). It has also been retold by David Adler in his picture book *The House on the Roof* in a present-day urban setting.

A Bird in the Hand—We first heard this story from Rabbi Avi Weiss, who told it at a 1992 Jewish story-telling conference at Stern College of Yeshiva University in New York City. We learned from Rabbi Weiss that he had used it in his sermons for many years, and that he had originally heard it from a fellow rabbi at the Laurel Park Hotel in Old South Falsberg, New York, when he was nineteen years old. The World War II setting is unique to our retelling for this book.

Hillel the Wise—This and other stories about Hillel were originally written down in a book of the Talmud called *Pirkei Avot—The Sayings of the Fathers.* Other versions can be found in William B. Silverman's *The Sages Speak: Rabbinic Wisdom and Jewish Values* (pp. 87–88); *The Encyclopedia Judaica* (vol. 8, p. 484), edited by Cecil Roth; and *Jewish Legends of the Second Commonwealth* (pp. 205–6) by Rabbi Judah Nadich.

Epilogue—This classic Hasidic tale has been passed on and retold by many authors and storytellers. It is in-cluded in Gershom C. Scholem's great scholarly work *Major Trends in Jewish Mysticism* (pp. 349–50). A ver-sion of it can be found in Elie Wiesel's *Souls on Fire:*

Portraits and Legends of Hasidic Masters (p. 167). Our version was inspired in large part by Barbara Myerhoff's retelling in *Number Our Days*. She attributes the story to "Moshe," one of the senior citizens she met at a center in Venice, California, which she studied and wrote about in her book.

If you are interested in finding out more about Jewish folklore and culture, you might want to join or write to any of these organizations:

THE JEWISH FOLKLORE SECTION OF THE AMERICAN FOLKLORE SOCIETY. They publish the *Jewish Folklore and Ethnology Review* and can be contacted at
Dept. of Judaic and Near Eastern Studies
Oberlin College
Oberlin, OH 44074

THE YIVO INSTITUTE FOR JEWISH RESEARCH
1048 Fifth Avenue
New York, NY 10028

THE JEWISH BOOK COUNCIL (sponsored by the Jewish Community Centers Association of North America)
15 East 26th Street
New York, NY 10010

The most extensive collection of worldwide Jewish folktales, founded and directed by Professor Dov Noy, is located at
THE ISRAEL FOLKTALE ARCHIVES
Haifa University
Haifa, Israel

Bibliography

Here are the books we used to research and learn about the stories:

Adler, David. *The House on the Roof: A Sukkot Story*. Rockville, MD: Kar-Ben Copies, Inc., 1984.

Ausubel, Nathan. *A Treasury of Jewish Folklore*. New York: Crown Publishers, 1948, 1975.

Boccaccio, Giovanni. *The Decameron*. Translated by Francis Winwar. New York: Random House, 1955.

Gaster, Moses. *The Ma'aseh Book*. Philadelphia: Jewish Publication Society, 1934.

Ginzberg, Louis. *Legends of the Jews,* Vol. I. Philadelphia: Jewish Publication Society, 1934.

Kogos, Fred. *1001 Yiddish Proverbs.* Secaucus, NJ: Citadel Press, 1980.

Kugelmass, Jack. *Miracle on Intervale Avenue.* New York: Schocken Books, 1986.

Leach, Maria. *Riddle Me, Riddle Me Ree.* New York: Viking Press, 1970.

Myerhoff, Barbara. *Number Our Days.* New York: E. P. Dutton, 1979.

Nadich, Judah. *Jewish Legends of the Second Commonwealth.* Philadelphia: Jewish Publication Society, 1983.

Nahmad, H. M. *A Portion in Paradise and Other Jewish Folktales.* New York: Schocken Books, 1974.

Novak, William, and Moshe Waldoks. *The Big Book of Jewish Humor.* New York: Harper and Row, 1981.

Noy, Dov. *Folktales of Israel.* Chicago: University of Chicago Press, 1963.

Petuchowski, Jacob J. *Our Masters Taught*. New York: Crossroad Publishing Co., 1982.

Roth, Cecil, ed. *The Encyclopedia Judaica*. Jerusalem: Keter Publishing House Ltd., 1972.

Rush, Barbara, and Eliezer Marcus. *Seventy and One Folktales for the Jewish Holidays and Festivals*. New York: American Zionist Youth Foundation, 1980.

Sanfield, Steve. *The Feather Merchants and Other Tales of the Fools of Chelm*. New York: Orchard Books, 1991.

Scholem, Gershom C. *Major Trends in Jewish Mysticism*. New York: Schocken Books, 1961.

Schram, Peninnah. *Jewish Stories: One Generation Tells Another*. Northvale, NJ: Jason Aronson, Inc., 1987.

Silverman, William B. *The Sages Speak: Rabbinic Wisdom and Jewish Values*. Northvale, NJ: Jason Aronson, Inc., 1989.

Simon, Maurice, trans. *Midrash Rabbah: Esther/Song of Songs*. New York: Soncinco Press, Ltd., 1983.

Weinreich, Beatrice Silverman, ed. *Yiddish Folktales.* New York: Random House, 1988.

Wiesel, Elie. *Souls on Fire: Portraits and Legends of Hasidic Masters.* New York: Random House, 1982.